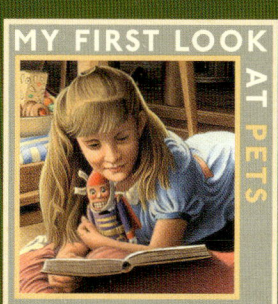

Rabbits are furry and long-eared animals

Rabbits

VALERIE BODDEN

Published by Creative Education

123 South Broad Street, Mankato, Minnesota 56001

Creative Education is an imprint of The Creative Company

Designed by Rita Marshall

Photographs by Getty Images (Wendy Ashton, Tim Davis, GK Hart / Vikki Hart, Catherine Ledner, Mahaux Photography, Paul McCormick, Neo Vision, Gary Randall, Steve Satushek, Joseph Van Os), photo on page 23 © BillMARCHEL.com

Copyright © 2007 Creative Education

International copyright reserved in all countries. No part of this book may be reproduced in any form without written permission from the publisher.

Printed in the United States of America

Library of Congress Cataloging-in-Publication Data

Bodden, Valerie. Rabbits / by Valerie Bodden.

p. cm. — (My first look at pets)

Includes bibliographical references and index.

ISBN-13 : 978-1-58341-460-6

1. Rabbits—Juvenile literature. I. Title. II. Series.

SF453.2.B63 2005   636.932'2—dc22   2005050687

First edition 9 8 7 6 5 4 3 2 1

Rabbits

Fun Bunnies 6

Choosing a Rabbit 8

Rabbit Care 12

Rabbit Fun 16

Hands-On: High Jumper 22

Additional Information 24

Fun Bunnies

Rabbits are playful animals that like to hop and wiggle their noses. Rabbits are also called "bunnies."

Rabbits have strong back legs and big front teeth. They have short tails and long ears. Most rabbits have ears that stand up. But some rabbits' ears hang down. Rabbits' big ears help them to hear well. Rabbits have a good sense of smell, too.

Rabbits use their ears to listen for danger

Rabbits are most active at the beginning and end of the day. They are usually quiet. But they can growl, grunt, and squeal. Rabbits thump their back feet on the ground if they are scared.

Choosing a Rabbit

There are many **breeds** of rabbits. They come in lots of colors. Some rabbits have black, white, brown, or gray fur. Other rabbits are more than one color. Some rabbits have long fur. Others have short fur.

Rabbits grind their teeth together or hop up and down when they are happy.

RABBITS OF ALL COLORS HAVE SOFT FUR

Pet rabbits come in many sizes. Some rabbits are small. They weigh less than three pounds (1.5 kg). Other rabbits are big. They can weigh as much as a small dog!

Some rabbits are wild. But many kinds of rabbits make good pets. Large and medium-sized rabbits are best for kids. Baby rabbits have lots of energy. Adult rabbits are calmer. They can be easier to care for.

A female rabbit is called a doe. A male rabbit is called a buck.

Wild rabbits do not make good pets

Rabbit Care

Pet rabbits should be kept in a **hutch**. The hutch needs to be at least four times as big as the rabbit. It should be cleaned often.

Rabbits need healthy food. They like to eat hay, **vegetables**, and **rabbit pellets**. They need fresh water, too.

Pet rabbits like to explore their homes

Rabbits do not need baths. But they do need to be brushed. Rabbits with long fur should be brushed every day. Rabbits' nails need to be trimmed, too.

Just like kids, rabbits need regular check-ups. A **veterinarian**, or vet, checks rabbits to make sure they are healthy. Most pet rabbits live 5 to 15 years.

Brushing keeps a rabbit's fur shiny

Rabbit Fun

Pet rabbits like to spend lots of time with their owners. Most rabbits like to be petted. Some rabbits like to sit next to people. But rabbits do not like to be picked up. If they have to be lifted, their whole body should be supported.

Rabbits need some time outside of their hutch every day. They like to hop around the house or the yard.

Fresh fruit, such as bits of apples or pears, makes a good treat for rabbits.

RABBITS LIKE PLAYTIME AND SNACK TIME

Rabbits enjoy spending time together

Rabbits like to play. Some rabbits like to roll little balls. Some like to play in paper bags or boxes. Others like to play with baby toys such as rattles. No matter what they are doing, rabbits like to know they are loved!

Rabbits need to be held carefully

Hands-on: High Jumper

Some rabbits can jump three feet (0.9 m) or higher. Can you jump that high?

What You Need

Some flour
A tape measure

What You Do

1. Dip your fingers in the flour.
2. Stand in front of a wall. Reach high above your head. Touch your fingers to the wall to leave a mark.
3. Dip your fingers in the flour again.
4. Stand in front of the wall. Jump as high as you can and touch the wall to leave another mark.
5. Measure the distance between the first and second marks. Did you jump as high as a rabbit?

Rabbits' strong legs help them jump high

Index

babies 10
breeds 8
ears 6
food 12, 17
fur 8, 14
hutch 12, 16
playing 20
size 10
veterinarian 14

Words to Know

breeds—kinds

hutch—a cage for a small animal such as a rabbit

rabbit pellets—a special kind of food made for rabbits; they are shaped like little vitamins

vegetables—plants that can be eaten; lettuce, broccoli, and celery are all vegetables

veterinarian—an animal doctor

Read More

Barnes, Julia. *101 Facts about Rabbits*. Milwaukee, Wis.: Gareth Stevens, 2001.

Foran, Jill. *Caring for Your Rabbit*. Mankato, Minn.: Weigl Publishers, 2003.

Ross, Veronica. *My First Rabbit*. North Mankato, Minn.: Thameside Press, 2002.

Explore the Web

Enchanted Learning: Rabbit http://www.enchantedlearning.com/subjects/mammals/farm/Rabbitprintout.shtml

Rabbit Care for Kids http://islandgems.net/rabbit_care_for_kids.html

Pet Care: Rabbit 411 http://www.animaland.org/asp/petcare/rabbit411.asp

**ERNESTVILLE-SALTSBURG
SCHOOL DISTRICT**

Date _____ No _____

Payment will be required
books lost or carelessly